PLANETARY
EXPLORATION

VENUS

SIMONE PAYMENT

Britannica®
Educational Publishing

IN ASSOCIATION WITH

ROSEN
EDUCATIONAL SERVICES

Published in 2017 by Britannica Educational Publishing (a trademark of Encyclopædia Britannica, Inc.) in association with The Rosen Publishing Group, Inc.
29 East 21st Street, New York, NY 10010

Distributed exclusively by Rosen Publishing.
To see additional Britannica Educational Publishing titles, go to rosenpublishing.com.

First Edition

Britannica Educational Publishing
J.E. Luebering: Executive Director, Core Editorial
Mary Rose McCudden: Editor, Britannica Student Encyclopedia

Rosen Publishing
Nicholas Croce: Editor
Nelson Sá: Art Director
Michael Moy: Designer
Cindy Reiman: Photography Manager
Bruce Donnola: Photo Researcher

Library of Congress Cataloging-in-Publication Data

Names: Payment, Simone.
Title: Venus / Simone Payment.
Description: New York : Britannica Educational Publishing in association with Rosen Educational Services, 2017. | Series: Planetary exploration | Includes bibliographical references and index.
Identifiers: LCCN 2016020884| ISBN 9781508103745 (library bound) | ISBN 9781508104100 (pbk) | ISBN 9781508103042 (6-pack)
Subjects: LCSH: Venus (Planet)—Juvenile literature. | Solar system—Juvenile literature.
Classification: LCC QB621 .P39 2017 | DDC 523.42—dc23
LC record available at https://lccn.loc.gov/2016020884

Manufactured in China

Photo credits: Cover Vadim Sadovski/Shutterstock.com (Venus); cover and interior pages background nienora/Shutterstock.com; p. 4 NASA/JAXA; p. 5, 10, 25 NASA/JPL; p. 6 NASA/Ames/JPL-Caltech; p. 7 Encyclopædia Britannica, Inc.; p. 8 Spencer Sutton/Science Source; p. 9 David A. Hardy/Science Source; p. 11 NASA/JPL/ESA; p. 12 JAXA/NASA/Hinode; p. 13 Stocktrek Images/Getty Images; p. 14 NASA/SDO; pp. 15, 22, 23, 27, 29 NASA; p. 16 Detlev van Ravensway/Science Source; p. 17, 21 NASA/JPL/Caltech; p. 18 Babak Tafreshi/National Geographic Image Collection/Getty Images; p. 19 Courtesy of L.D. Travis and W.B. Rossow; p. 20 U.S. Naval Observatory Library; p. 24 Courtesy of C.M. Pieters through the Brown/Vernadsky Institute to Institute Agreement and the U.S.S.R. Academy of Sciences, and C.M. Pieters et al. "The Color of the Surface of Venus," Science, vol. 234, p. 1382, Dec. 12, 1986, copyright © 1986 by the American Association for the Advancement of Science; p. 26 NASA/Goddard Space Flight Center; p. 28 dpa picture alliance archive/Alamy Stock Photo.

CONTENTS

VENUS, THE HOTTEST PLANET

Venus is one of the planets that orbit, or travel around, the sun in our **solar system**. Venus is the second planet from the sun. Its distance from the sun averages about 67 million miles (108 million kilometers). Venus is the hottest planet in the solar system. Like the planet Mercury, Venus has no moon.

Venus is the brightest planet in the sky when viewed from Earth. It is

Venus can be seen in the night sky above Earth from the International Space Station.

VOCABULARY

The **solar system** is made up of the sun and all of the planets, moons, asteroids, and comets that travel around the sun.

Earth's nearest neighbor, coming closer to Earth than any other planet.

Of all the planets in our solar system, Venus is the most similar to Earth in size and other features. This makes scientists think the two planets might have similar histories. Today, Earth and Venus are very different. Scientists are hoping to someday find out why.

The Pioneer Venus Orbiter (Pioneer 12) spacecraft took this photo of Venus in February 1979.

HOW BIG IS VENUS?

Venus is about the same size and weight as Earth. Its diameter, or the distance through its center, is about 7,521 miles (12,104 km). Earth's diameter is 7,926 miles (12,756 km).

Venus is also similar in size to some of the other planets that have been found outside our solar system. However, it is small if you compare it

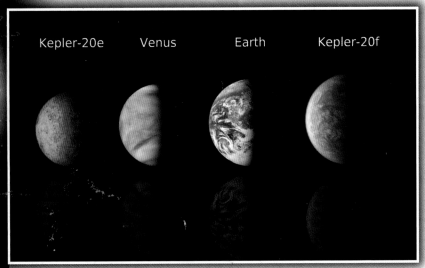

Kepler-20e   Venus   Earth   Kepler-20f

Venus is similar in size to Earth as well as to at least two planets that are outside the solar system.

COMPARE AND CONTRAST

Venus and Earth are sometimes called twin planets or sister planets. Compare how the two planets are similar and how they are different.

to the largest planet in the solar system, which is Jupiter. Jupiter has a diameter of 88,846 miles (142,984 km). That is more than eleven times longer than Venus's diameter. In fact, more than 1,300 planets the size of Venus would fit inside Jupiter. Jupiter is so large that it has two and a half times more mass, or amount of matter within it, than all the other planets in the solar system put together.

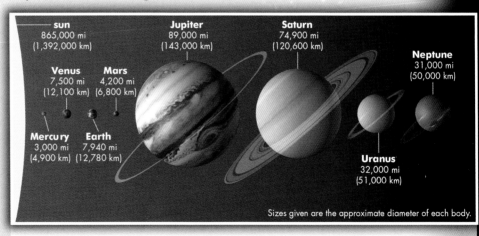

sun
865,000 mi
(1,392,000 km)

Jupiter
89,000 mi
(143,000 km)

Saturn
74,900 mi
(120,600 km)

Neptune
31,000 mi
(50,000 km)

Venus
7,500 mi
(12,100 km)

Mars
4,200 mi
(6,800 km)

Mercury
3,000 mi
(4,900 km)

Earth
7,940 mi
(12,780 km)

Uranus
32,000 mi
(51,000 km)

Sizes given are the approximate diameter of each body.

This illustration shows just how small Venus is compared to the giant planets, Jupiter and Saturn.

INSIDE THE PLANET

Scientists are not exactly sure what the interior of Venus is like. Because Venus is very similar to Earth, they think the interior is probably solid and rocky. Scientists believe that Venus also has layers like Earth's. These layers are made up of a metal core, a thick rocky middle, and a crust.

Like Earth, Venus probably has a core that is made of iron and nickel. The middle layer of a planet, called the mantle, is the thickest part of

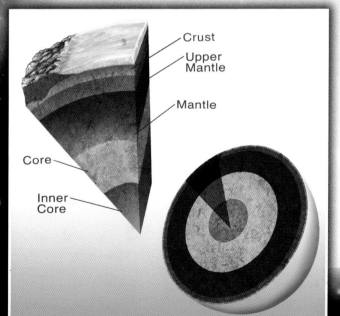

Crust

Upper Mantle

Mantle

Core

Inner Core

Scientists think that Venus has layers like Earth's layers, which are shown here.

THINK ABOUT IT

Many of Venus's surface features have been caused by volcanoes. How might this information help scientists understand the inside of Venus?

Venus. It is about 1,900 miles (3,000 km) thick. It is probably made up of rock and hot melted rock. The crust of a planet is its outer layer. Venus's crust is rocky. It is probably about 19 miles (30 km) thick.

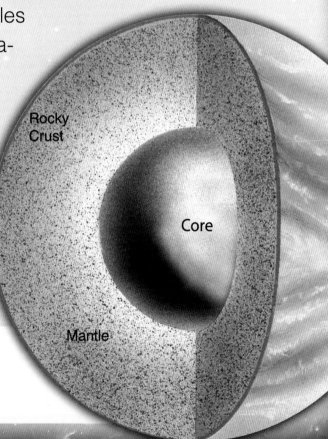

Rocky Crust

Core

Mantle

Scientists think that Venus's mantle is probably the thickest part of its interior.

ON THE SURFACE

Venus's surface is dry and rocky. There are plains, craters, and mountains. There are also more than 1,000 volcanoes.

Like other planets, Venus has craters that were formed when **asteroids** from space hit the planet's surface. Venus's craters are all at least about a mile (1.6 km) across. This is because the thick, hot air surrounding Venus causes smaller asteroids to slow down and break apart before they can hit the surface of the planet.

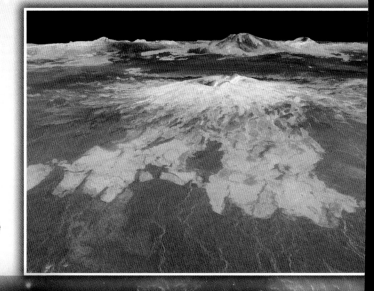

Sapas Mons is one of Venus's many volcanoes. It is almost 1 mile (1.6 km) high.

Venus has several mountain ranges. The tallest mountain range on Venus is Maxwell Montes. It is about 7 miles (11 km) tall. Mount Everest, the tallest mountain on Earth, is only 5.5 miles (8.8 km) high. Venus also has tall volcanoes. The tallest is called Maat Mons. It is about the same height as Mount Everest and is similar in shape and size to the largest island of Hawaii.

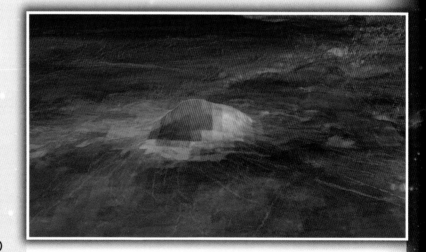

This image shows Venus's volcano Idunn Mons. The reddish-orange area near its summit is where there is the most heat.

VENUS'S THICK ATMOSPHERE

Although Venus is not the closest planet to the sun, it is the hottest planet in the solar system. This is because the layer of gases surrounding Venus, or Venus's atmosphere, is thick and heavy. Also, thick clouds cover the planet. The gases and clouds trap heat. When an atmosphere traps energy from the sun like this, it is called the greenhouse effect. Venus has the most powerful greenhouse effect in the solar system. The average temperature at Venus's surface is about 867° F (464° C).

With the sun in the background, the atmosphere of Venus glows yellow around the planet.

How does Earth's atmosphere compare with Venus's atmosphere?

Venus's atmosphere is made up mostly of carbon dioxide gas. It also contains nitrogen and small amounts of water vapor and other gases. As a comparison, Earth's atmosphere contains mostly water vapor and the gases nitrogen and oxygen. Venus also has thick clouds of sulfur dioxide gas and sulfuric acid. These clouds give Venus its yellowish color. The clouds are blown around the planet by winds stronger than any hurricane on Earth. They move at about 220 miles (350 km) per hour.

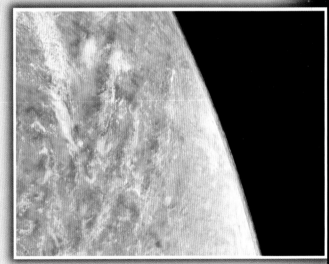

Venus's thick cloud covering makes it difficult for astronomers to view the planet's surface.

AROUND THE SUN

Like all planets, Venus has two types of motion: orbit and spin. The orbit is the path a planet takes as it travels around the sun. All eight planets revolve around the sun in elliptical, or oval-shaped, orbits. Venus's orbit is the most nearly circular of all the planets.

Venus's orbit is shorter than Earth's because it is closer to the sun. Venus takes 225 Earth days to complete one orbit. In other words, one year on Venus lasts 225 Earth days.

This image contains a series of photos that show Venus crossing the sun during its transit in 2012.

Sometimes Venus passes between Earth and the sun. This occasion is a type of eclipse called a transit. Venus then appears to observers on Earth as a small black circle crossing the sun. Two transits of Venus occur about every 125 years. The last two transits occurred in 2004 and 2012. The next transit will not take place until 2117.

A special filter was used on the camera that took this photo of the 2012 transit of Venus.

A STRANGE SPIN

Venus also spins, or rotates around its center. A planet's orbit and spin combine in a complex way to determine the length of a day on that planet. Earth completes one spin in twenty-four hours, or one day. Venus spins much more slowly. It takes 243 Earth days to make a complete spin.

Venus is unusual because the length of its day is different from the time it takes to complete one rotation. A day on a planet is the time it takes for the sun to appear straight overhead, to set, and then to rise straight

A day on Venus, the time it takes for the sun to appear overhead, set, and appear overhead again, is equal to about 117 Earth days.

On Earth, the sun appears to rise in the east and set in the west. In what direction would the sun appear to rise to an observer on Venus?

overhead again. One day on Venus lasts about 117 Earth days.

Another unusual fact about Venus is that it spins in the opposite direction of Earth and five other planets in the solar system. Uranus also spins clockwise about its north pole. Scientists are not sure why Venus spins this way.

Radar images like this one allow scientists to see beneath Venus's thick clouds and track how long Venus takes to complete one rotation.

ANCIENT OBSERVATIONS

People in ancient times noticed that many twinkling points of light in the night sky followed the same predictable path. The lights also stayed in a fixed position with respect to one another. What ancient people were observing were the stars. In comparison, some points of light that did not twinkle followed very complicated paths across the sky. These points of light would change direction and did not stay in fixed positions with respect to other points of light. Ancient

At some times of the year Venus appears in the hours before sunrise. At other times it can be seen in the hours after sunset.

THINK ABOUT IT

Only one object in Earth's night sky can appear to be brighter than Venus. Which object do you think it is?

people named these moving points of light "planets." The word "planet" comes from the Greek word *planetes*, which means "wanderers."

Even thousands of years ago, long before telescopes were invented, people could see Venus from Earth. The clouds surrounding Venus reflected the light from the sun, as they do now. From Earth, that makes Venus look very bright. Perhaps because of the planet's jewel-like appearance, Venus was eventually named after the Roman goddess of love and beauty.

This image shows the V-shaped patterns that form as strong winds blow clouds around Venus.

EARLY STUDIES OF THE PLANET

By the early 1600s several people had made simple telescopes. These allowed people to see distant objects more clearly. The Italian **astronomer** Galileo Galilei was the first person to observe Venus with a telescope.

In the 1700s and 1800s, stronger telescopes allowed astronomers to study Venus more closely. However, Venus's thick cloud coverage prevented scientists from viewing the planet's surface features.

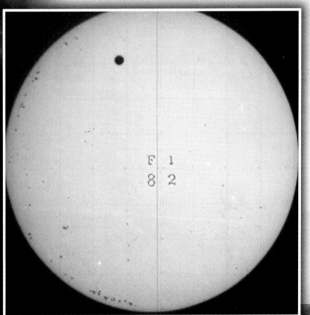

In 1882 astronomers took this photograph using a telescope. It shows Venus crossing the sun during a transit.

In the 1900s a new technology was developed that allowed astronomers to study Venus's surface. That technology was radar. Radar bounces radio waves off of objects. Scientists measure the time it takes for the wave to come back. Computers then create a picture from that information. This amazing technology helped astronomers "see" the tall mountains that exist on Venus.

This radar image shows Venus's surface. Low regions are colored violet. High regions are in pink and red.

FLYING BY VENUS

Since the 1960s more than 20 unmanned spacecraft have visited, flown by, or orbited Venus. The National Aeronautics and Space Administration (NASA) launched the

Mariner 2 spacecraft in August 1962. When it reached Venus a few months later, it became the first spacecraft to fly near another planet and return data. Mariner 2 collected data about the planet's rotation and extremely high surface temperatures.

In 1967 another spacecraft called Mariner 5 flew closer to Venus. It returned more precise data about

This is the Mariner 5 spacecraft before it was launched in 1967. It passed by Venus at a distance of about 2,500 miles (4,000 km).

COMPARE AND CONTRAST

What might astronomers have learned from spacecraft flying by Venus that they could not have learned from using radar or telescopes?

the atmosphere, including the amount of carbon dioxide there. In 1974 Mariner 10 took about 4,000 photographs of Venus during a flyby. It captured images of Venus's clouds.

In 1978 two spacecraft, called Pioneer Venus 1 and Pioneer Venus 2 arrived at the planet. Pioneer Venus 1 mapped Venus's surface and continued to orbit Venus for 14 years. Pioneer Venus 2 released four unmanned spacecraft called probes to collect data at different points in the planet's atmosphere.

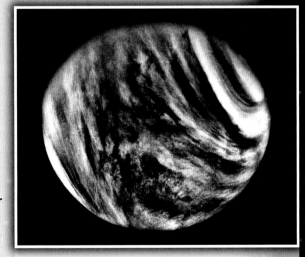

The Mariner 10 spacecraft took this close-up photo of Venus in 1974.

TOUCHDOWN

In 1970, the Soviet Union's Venera 7 spacecraft landed on Venus. It was the first spacecraft to successfully land on another planet. Other Venera missions sent more landers to Venus. Venera 9 and Venera 10 sent close-up photographs of the surface of Venus. These were the first photographs taken from the surface of another planet.

This photo was taken by the Venera 13 lander in 1982. It shows the rocky surface of Venus. Parts of the spacecraft are visible in the lower half of the image.

THINK ABOUT IT

Why do you think that the first planet that spacecraft from Earth flew by and landed on was Venus?

However, none of the spacecraft that landed on Venus lasted for long. The spacecraft were destroyed by the extreme heat and pressure on the surface. The Venera 12 mission lasted the longest. It managed to send information back to Earth for almost two hours, but then it burned up.

The last two missions were Venera 15 and Venera 16. They launched from Earth in 1983. Both spacecraft were orbiters that used radar to map about a quarter of Venus's surface, mostly around its north pole.

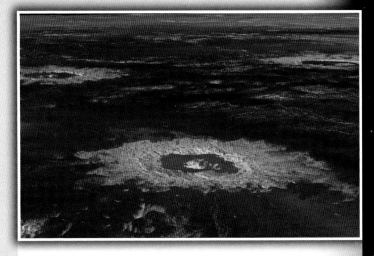

Venus has several craters on its surface. They are probably from meteorites hitting the planet sometime in the past.

MAGELLAN AND THE VENUS EXPRESS

In 1989 NASA launched the spacecraft Magellan from a space shuttle. Magellan arrived at Venus in 1990 and orbited the planet every three hours for the next four years. Magellan mapped the planet's cloud-covered surface in great detail.

The first European mission to Venus was the orbiter Venus Express. The European Space Agency (ESA) launched the

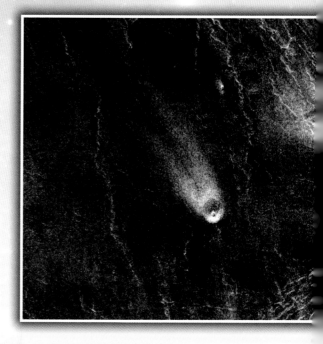

The Magellan spacecraft took this radar image of a small volcano on Venus in 1991.

spacecraft in 2005. It began orbiting Venus in 2006 to study the planet's **environment**, atmosphere, and surface. Venus Express observed small amounts of water and other evidence that suggested that oceans may have existed on Venus long ago. The spacecraft also returned the first images of cloud structures over the planet's south pole.

The Venus Express also took pictures of Earth from its orbit around Venus. Astronomers use these observations of Earth to consider what life on Earth may appear like to planets that exist outside of our solar system.

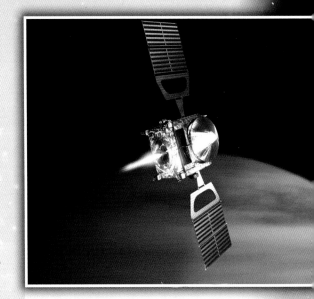

The Venus Express mission lasted longer than planned. Eventually the spacecraft burned up in Venus's atmosphere.

INTO THE FUTURE

In spite of Venus's intense surface heat and pressure, scientists have been able to send spacecraft there and find out much about the planet. Though it is unlikely that people will ever be able to land on Venus, they may figure out a way to take a closer look.

NASA has several plans for exploring Venus over a long period of time. According to one plan, astronauts would be onboard spacecraft within Venus's atmosphere! However, the spacecraft would

Plans for a mission named BepiColombo call for it to fly by Venus on its way to Mercury.

Venus has the most powerful greenhouse effect in the solar system. How might learning more about Venus's greenhouse effect help people understand and improve Earth's atmosphere?

remain at a height of 31 miles (50 km) above Venus's hot surface. At that height the pressure and temperature are like those of Earth. From there, astronauts may be able to study Venus up close. There is still much more to learn about Earth's nearest neighbor.

NASA astronaut Scott Kelly took this photo of Earth, the moon, and Venus from the International Space Station.

GLOSSARY

AERONAUTICS The science of flight and operation of aircraft.

CARBON DIOXIDE A colorless, odorless gas that is essential for life. Plants use carbon dioxide to make the food they need. Carbon dioxide in the air helps trap energy from the sun to warm Earth's surface.

COMET A small chunk of dust and ice that orbits the sun.

CORE The center part of a planet.

CRATER A hole made by an impact (as of a meteorite).

DIAMETER A straight line passing through the center of a figure or body.

GODDESS A female god.

IRON A heavy magnetic silver-white metallic element.

LANDER A type of spacecraft that lands on the surface of a planet or moon.

LEAD A soft, heavy metallic element.

MANTLE The middle layer of a planet between the crust (surface) and the core (center).

MOLTEN Melted by extreme heat.

NICKEL A silver-white hard metallic element.

NITROGEN A colorless, odorless element that exists naturally as a gas on Earth and makes up about 78 percent of Earth's atmosphere.

PLAIN A broad area of level or rolling treeless country.

PRESSURE A measure of the amount of force applied by something to something else in direct contact with it.

RADAR A device that sends out radio waves for detecting and locating an object by the reflection of the radio waves.

RANGE A series of mountains in a line.

ROTATION One complete turn around an axis or center.

SULFUR DIOXIDE A heavy, strong-smelling gas.

SULFURIC ACID A heavy oily strong acid that is colorless when pure and eats away at many solid substances.

FOR MORE INFORMATION

Books

Graham, Ian. *Planets Near Earth*. Mankato, MN: Smart Apple Media, 2015.

Kazunas, Ariel. *Venus*. Ann Arbor, MI: Cherry Lake Publishers, 2012.

Lawrence, Ellen. *Venus: The Hot and Toxic Planet*. St. Austell, UK: Ruby Tuesday Books, 2014.

Reilly, Carmel. *The Planets*. New York, NY: Marshall Cavendish, 2012.

Ring, Susan. *Venus*. New York, NY: Weigl, 2014.

Websites

Because of the changing nature of internet links, Rosen Publishing has developed an online list of websites related to the subject of this book. This site is updated regularly. Please use this link to access the list:

http://www.rosenlinks.com/PE/venus

INDEX

523.42 P
Payment, Simone.
Venus /

FLT

06/17